EX LIBRIS

THIS BOOK BELONGS TO:

WARNING! DO NOT USE YOUR REAL NAME!

"LIKE MOST PEOPLE, QUINN
KNEW ALMOST NOTHING ABOUT
CRIME... WHAT INTERESTED
HIM ABOUT THE STORIES HE
WROTE WAS NOT THEIR RELATION
TO THE WORLD BUT THEIR RELATION
TO OTHER STORIES."
- PAUL AUSTER, CITY OF GLASS

A NOTE ON THE ART

Astute readers may notice that sometimes an object described as having a certain color is shown in the pictures to have a different color. A blood-red letter might look black. Blue bits on a flag might be orange. A gold harp appears green. That's because we only use three kinds of ink to print the artwork in these books: black, orange, and green. So everything in this book, no matter what color it is in real life, looks black, orange, or green. Or white! That's where we didn't use any ink at all. You probably didn't need a note explaining all this. But you never know, you know?

—M.B.

For Liza B.
—M.B.

To my brother, Jon, who joined me in running out of the theater during *Gremlins*.
—M.L.

MAC B.

KID SPY

THE IMPOSSIBLE CRIME

By **Mac Barnett**

Illustrated by **Mike Lowery**

Orchard Books
New York
An Imprint of Scholastic Inc.

ME AS A

~~KID~~

SPY!

FROM THE DESK OF

MAC BARNETT

MY NAME IS MAC BARNETT.
I AM AN AUTHOR. BUT
BEFORE I WAS AN
AUTHOR, I WAS A KID.
AND WHEN I WAS A
KID, I WAS A SPY.

AN AUTHOR'S JOB IS TO
MAKE UP STORIES. BUT
THE STORY YOU ARE
ABOUT TO READ IS TRUE.

THIS ACTUALLY HAPPENED
TO ME.

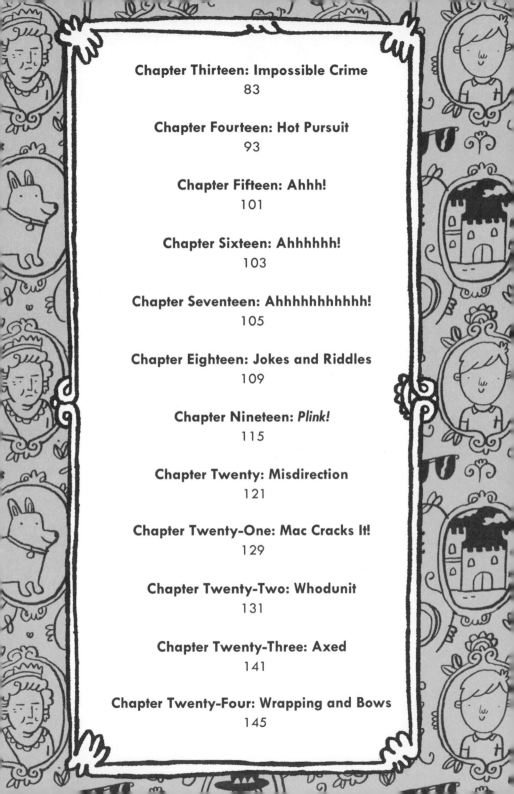

It was 1989. It was Saturday.

I was somewhere I spent many Saturdays in 1989: Golden Tee Golfland.

Golden Tee Golfland is a real place, on a real street called Castro Valley Boulevard, in a real town called Castro Valley. You can look it up.

Golden Tee Golfland is a real mini-golf course, full of all the fake stuff you find at real mini-golf courses: real fake windmills, real fake pagodas, and three real fake dragons whose long necks poke out from a volcano.

Castro Valley is in California, a place with warm sun and wide blue sky. It is almost always nice to be outside, which is great if you love mini-golf.

When I was a kid, I liked mini-golf OK.

But I loved video games.

And Golden Tee Golfland had an arcade.

Outside the arcade it was a fine spring day.

Inside the arcade it was dark and smelled like old carpet. Above a counter in the corner, there was a pink neon sign that said SNACK BAR. They sold pizza slices for a buck. (The pizza wasn't good.) Plastic air hockey pucks clacked against tables. Hard rubber balls rolled up Skee-Ball alleys and thudded into the gutters. Machines beeped.

Kids screamed. Machines booped. Kids screamed some more. There was an area with games that spit out long strands of tickets you could trade in for plastic prizes: fake spiders, Super Balls. The prizes were cheap. Ticket games were for suckers. I was there to play video games, where a quarter got you three lives and the only prize was a place on the high-score list. You didn't play for Super Balls. You played to be the best.

Game cabinets stood in neat rows, like columns in a ruined temple. Their screens glowed. The words INSERT COIN flashed in the darkness. I was in the corner, past ALTERED BEAST, past EXCALIBUR, past TEENAGE MUTANT NINJA TURTLES and GHOULS 'N GHOSTS.

Those games were all good. But I was playing
SPY MASTER 2: ARCADE EDITION.

SPY MASTER 2: ARCADE EDITION was the
arcade-only sequel to SPY MASTER. The graphics
were better. The missions were crazier. But mostly
the game was famous for being really, really hard.
Impossible. Unbeatable.

And there I was, on the final boss, with three
lives and a power-up.

Behind me, I heard someone say, "Hey, this kid's
going to beat SPY MASTER 2!"

Jump. Punch. Jump. Jump. Punch. I'd been hunched over the controls for three hours, sweating and smashing buttons. When my mom dropped me off at Golfland that morning, she'd handed me a five-dollar bill. I'd changed four bucks to quarters and spent the last dollar on a slice of pizza. The greasy plate was still perched on top of the game cabinet.

A crowd had formed behind me.

"He's still got three lives," said a kid.

"And a power-up," said another kid.

"I've never seen anyone beat this game," said a forty-year-old man in a tank top who was always in the arcade.

I tried to block out the commotion. The final boss of SPY MASTER 2 was the Spy Master himself, a giant KGB agent who wore a black suit and carried a metal briefcase. The showdown took place on the wing of a Russian airplane.

I was pounding away on the jump button, dodging the Spy Master's attacks.

"Hey, what's your name, dude?" somebody asked.

"Mac." I didn't take my eyes off the screen.

"Matt?"

This happened to me a lot.

"Mac," I said. "M-A-C."

"Hey, that's only three letters! You can put your whole name on the high score list!"

That was true. It was the best thing about having a three-letter name in the 1980s. And if I beat the game, I would have the number-one high score. Anybody who came to Golden Tee Golfland would know I was the best.

The Spy Master threw a stick of dynamite. I jumped over it and landed a punch on his belly.

The crowd was chanting my name.

"He's gonna beat it!" the man in the tank top shouted.

"Rad!" said a kid.

"Nah. He'll choke."

I recognized that voice.

It was Derek Lafoy.

Derek Lafoy went to my school. He called me "Mac Barn Head." He threw my gym shoes on the roof of the school. He owned a pet snake, which he kept in a red, glowing, glass box in the corner of his room. I had heard about the snake from kids who had seen it. I had never been to Derek's house. He never invited me to his birthday parties. (If he had, I would have gone.)

"Derek," I said. "What are you doing here?"

"I'm having my birthday party," he said.

"Oh," I said.

I risked looking up from the game and recognized a lot of my classmates in the crowd around me. Tiffany. Brandon. Hendrick. Both Ashleys.

This could be my moment of glory. I had to win.

The Spy Master was throwing poison darts. Jump. Jump. Jump.

"MAC! MAC! MAC!" chanted the crowd.

"MATT! MATT! MATT!" chanted a couple kids in the crowd.

"CHOKE! CHOKE! CHOKE!" chanted Derek Lafoy.

Now the Spy Master's suitcase was glowing.

"Why is it glowing?" asked Mr. Tank Top.

"Uh-oh," said a kid.

Now Derek was the only one chanting. "CHOKE! CHOKE!"

Twelve rays of light burst from the Spy Master's suitcase and the screen went white.

"Aw, man! He used a nuke!"

I had never seen anything like it.

All three of my lives were wiped out.

The Spy Master put on a pair of sunglasses and laughed.

A countdown clock popped up. I had ten seconds to put in another quarter and continue.

TIME REMAINING: 10

I reached into my pocket.

There was nothing but the napkin that came with my pizza.

TIME REMAINING: 6

"Told you he'd choke," said Derek Lafoy.

I took out my wallet and undid the Velcro. Maybe I could make it to the change machine and back in six seconds.

I was out of money.

TIME REMAINING: 2

"Hey, does anyone have a quarter?" I asked.

But the crowd that had grown around me was gone now.

TIME REMAINING: 0

The screen flashed the saddest two words in the English language:

I was stunned.

I checked my watch.

My mom was on a movie date with her boyfriend, Craig. Craig always took my mom to the afternoon shows because he thought only suckers paid full price for movie tickets. My mom wasn't supposed to pick me up for another half hour.

What was I supposed to do for all that time?

I decided I would go outside and watch people golf. (The saddest ten words in the English language.)

I pushed the door open and stepped into the daylight.

It took a minute for my eyes to adjust.

But when I did, I saw something strange by the eighteenth hole.

The eighteenth hole had a fake castle with a moat and drawbridge.

That wasn't the strange thing.

The strange thing was a real dog standing on the drawbridge, wearing a backpack and holding a scroll in his mouth.

"Freddie!" I said.

The dog noticed me and began furiously wagging his tail.

"Is this your dog?" asked an angry dad, who had to hit his ball over the drawbridge to get to the hole.

"No," I said. "Well, yes. No. Sort of."

"Well get him out of the way!" the dad shouted.

But Freddie was already out of the way.

He was running over to me.

"No dogs allowed at Golfland!" the dad said.

"Just play, Dennis," said the mom. "You're upsetting Zachary."

Freddie lifted his head and offered me the scroll.

I took it from his mouth and unrolled it.

Freddie's mouth was wet, and the ink on the scroll had run. But I could still read it.

"What phone?" I asked.
To my right, a pay phone started ringing.
I picked up Freddie.
Then I picked up the phone.
It was the Queen of England.

"Hello," I said.

"Hullo," said the Queen. "May I speak to Mac?"

"Speaking," I said.

"Mac, I have an important favor to ask you."

"Let me guess," I said. "Someone took the Crown Jewels."

"Let me speak," said the Queen. "No."

"Oh," I said.

Usually when the Queen of England called me, it was because someone took the Crown Jewels.

I smiled. "Did you call to say hello?"

"Of course not," said the Queen. "Do you really think I would make a long-distance call just to say hullo? What is that awful racket behind you?"

"I'm at a mini-golf course," I said.

"A what what course?" said the Queen.

"A mini-golf course," I said.

"I do not know what that is," said the Queen. "And I do not care to know."

I felt a bit defensive.

"It's like golf, but shrunken down," I said.

"With lots of obstacles and castles and stuff."

"Real castles?"

"No, mini-castles."

"Ah," said the Queen. "Sounds dreadful."

"I'm just here to play arcade games."

"I see," said the Queen. "Even worse."

"I've been trying to beat this one game for like a month," I said.

"And did you beat it?"

"No," I said. "It's impossible."

The Queen frowned.

(I could tell she was frowning, even over the phone.)

"Nothing is impossible," said the Queen.

"Well," I said, "it's really, really, really hard."

"Then why do you play?" the Queen asked.

"It's a great game!" I said.

"Mac," said the Queen, "I did not call to talk to you about a great game. I called to talk to you about *the* great game."

I waited while the Queen paused dramatically.

"International spycraft!" said the Queen.

"OK," I said.

"Mac," said the Queen, "you must come to England at once. Someone is about to steal the Crown Jewels!"

"I knew it was about the Crown Jewels!" I said. "Who wants to steal them? A KGB man?"

"No," said the Queen. "An *Irishman*."

"I'm part Irish!" I said.

"That is obvious," said the Queen. "Your name is Mac. Now, Mac, do you accept this mission?"

"Nobody is going to steal my pants, are they?"

The Queen began coughing horribly. "I beg your pardon?" she said.

"The first time I went on one of these missions, somebody stole my best pair of blue jeans."

(That's true. You can look it up in *Mac B., Kid Spy #1: Mac Undercover.*)

"Ah!" said the Queen. "Your *trousers.* In Britain, 'pants' means 'underwear.'"

A LESSON IN BRITISH ENGLISH

= PANTS

= TROUSERS

"Oh," I said. "That's good to know."

"Indeed," said the Queen. "In any case, I make no promises. You are a secret agent. You are responsible for your own trousers."

"And pants!" I said.

"That is not funny," said the Queen.

There was a click.

I set Freddie on the ground, and he immediately began licking a nearby windmill.

"She hung up," I said.

I stood there, not knowing what to do next.

At a nearby picnic table, a bunch of kids in my class were sitting around an ice-cream cake. Derek Lafoy cut into the cake, and then licked the knife.

"Mmmm, *ice cold!*" he said.

My classmates laughed.

I didn't get it.

The phone rang. Again.

It was the Queen of England. Again.

"Hello," I said.

"Hullo," said the Queen. "May I speak to Mac?"

"Speaking," I said.

"What is that singing in the background?"

"Oh, some kids are singing 'Happy Birthday' to Derek Lafoy."

"Oh!" said the Queen. "Why didn't you say you were at a birthday party?"

"I'm not."

"Ah," said the Queen. "Well, may I speak to Freddie?"

I called Freddie over and placed the phone to his ear. I could hear the Queen give a muffled command.

Freddie stuck his snout into his backpack and dug around. He pulled out an envelope and wagged while he held it in his mouth.

I opened the envelope, because I was Mac Barnett.

(I still am.)

Inside was a plane ticket and a stack of colorful British money.

I wondered if the arcade would exchange British money for American quarters.

They wouldn't, so Freddie and I took a taxi to the airport.

3

SPY LIFE

That is how it happens.

One minute you are waiting for your mom to pick you up from a mini-golf course in California. The next minute you are flying to England on a secret mission to protect the Crown Jewels.

I know. It does not make much sense.

But when I think back on the many years I spent being a kid, things like this happened a lot: Grown-ups were always making me do things that did not make much sense.

Maybe life is different for you. I hope so. But I have a feeling you know what I mean.

This is Buckingham Palace.

It is one of many palaces owned by the Queen of England.

Buckingham Palace is a very nice place to live. It has:

240 BEDROOMS

78 BATHROOMS

AND A BIG FLAGPOLE.

39 ACRES OF GARDENS

SEVERAL NICE VASES

When the Queen is home, this flag flies from the roof:

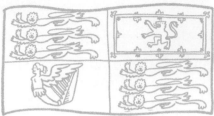

(It is the Royal Standard, the Queen's own flag.)
When the Queen is staying somewhere else, at one of her other castles, this flag flies from the roof:

(It is the Union Jack, the flag of Great Britain.)
When I passed through the gates in front of Buckingham Palace in the backseat of a swift black car, I looked up and saw this flag.

Frowning men in suits ushered me through a tall door, and through many more doors, until I arrived in a large pink-and-blue room. "Please wait here, Mr. Barnett," said one of the frowning men. "The Queen will see you momentarily." He smoothed his suit and disappeared through a tall door.

I was alone.

When I was a kid, I was very small, the smallest kid in my class. The pink-and-blue room made me feel even smaller. That one room was bigger than my whole house, and had more chairs too.

I thought about having a seat, but the chairs did not look like anyone had ever sat in them. So I just looked at some old paintings instead.

There were pictures of women with crowns:

Men with dogs:

And kids with goat legs.

(I liked those pictures best.)

Halfway around the room I stumbled across a table with a nice vase and a bowl of hard candies.

I was very hungry. I hadn't eaten since the slice of pizza in the arcade. And so I decided to help myself to one.

After I unwrapped the candy, but before I could pop it into my mouth, a tall door opened nearby. Another frowning man entered and frowned harder.

"Please replace the candy in its bowl and follow me to the Corgi Room."

5

THE CORGI
ROOM

In my life I have seen many strange things.

But nothing is stranger than what I saw in the
Corgi Room.

The Corgi Room contained eleven wicker baskets,
and ten of the baskets contained a corgi.

Some of the corgis were curled up and sleeping.

Some of them sniffed, and some of them scratched.

Some of them pointed their snouts in the air and yapped.

In the middle of the room, the Queen of England, dressed in red from hat to shoes, stood and gazed fondly at her dogs.

When Freddie saw the Queen, he ran up and began licking her ankle.

"To bed, Freddie," said the Queen.

He gave her leg one last lick and hopped into the empty basket.

Finally, the Queen faced me.

I bowed.

"What are you doing?" asked the Queen.

"Bowing," I said.

The Queen rolled her eyes.

"That is not how you bow."

"I'm trying my best," I said.

"Hmmm," said the Queen.

"I don't really know how to bow!" I said. "I'm from California!"

"I am aware of that," said the Queen. "It is one of my least favorite things about you."

At that moment, a wonderful smell wafted into the Corgi Room.

At the next moment, a graceful butler wafted into the room as well. He was holding a silver tray piled with beautifully patterned bowls heaped with steaming food. He placed his tray down atop a gold table. I couldn't stop staring at it.

"Seared and diced fillet steak," said the butler, "poached pheasant over steamed and lightly spiced rice, and grilled leg of rabbit with finely chopped cabbage. A beef gravy tonight, Your Majesty." He frowned, bowed, and left.

It sounded delicious.

"Excellent," said the Queen. "You have arrived just in time for dinner."

"That *is* excellent!" I said.

"I was speaking to Freddie. Corgis, line up!"

The dogs formed a half circle around the Queen and sat, staring up at her.

She picked up the gravy boat, and holding one pinky out, poured a little in each bowl. Then she set down a bowl of steak in front of a corgi with gray fur.

"Agatha, you may eat."

Agatha ate.

The Queen turned to me.

"Agatha is thirteen years old," the Queen explained. "The dogs eat in order of seniority."

When Agatha had eaten her steak, the Queen gently laid a bowl of rabbit before the next dog.

"You may eat, Simon," said the Queen.

Simon ate.

One by one, oldest to youngest, the Queen fed her eleven dogs. This is how the Queen's corgis ate dinner each night. That's true. You can look it up.

When Freddie finished, the Queen said, "Corgis! To bed!" and they all returned to their baskets.

I had hoped there would be some food left over. There wasn't.

The Queen smiled at me.

"Now," she said, "what important lesson have

you learned from what you just saw?"

"Always pack snacks on a long trip?" I said.

"Incorrect," said the Queen. "Respect your elders."

"Oh," I said. "OK."

"But Mac," said the Queen. "I did not bring you to England to teach you important lessons. You are here to protect the Crown Jewels. For tonight someone will *attempt* to steal them!"

I gasped, even though she had kind of already told me that on the phone.

"Who is going to steal them?" I asked.

"Nobody, I should hope."

"You know what I meant," I said.

"Ask your question more precisely," said the Queen.

"Who is going to *attempt* to steal them?" I asked.

"That is the wrong question," said the Queen. "The question is not *who*, but *why*?"

"What?"

The Queen pulled a piece of paper from her red purse.

"I received this letter in yesterday's post," she said.

The letter was written in bright red ink.

TOMORROW NIGHT
I WILL GET WHAT
MY GREAT-GREAT-GREAT-
GREAT-GREAT-GREAT-
GREAT-GREAT-GREAT-
GREAT GRANDFATHER
DID NOT. I WILL NOT
BE STOPPED. WE HAVE
BEEN WAITING 318 YEARS!

"Wow," I said.

"Indeed," said the Queen.

"I still don't get it," I said.

The Queen sighed.

"I shall tell you a story. A true story. In 1671—"

"Oh boy," I said.

"*In 1671,*" said the Queen, "a very bad man did a very bad thing. The man's name was Thomas Blood. He was known throughout England as

"Good name," I said.

"Colonel Blood was a handsome man and a smooth talker, a rebel, a kidnapper, an Irishman, and a secret agent for the King of England."

"He was a lot of things," I said.

"We are all of us a lot of things," said the Queen. "Another thing Blood was, was a jewel thief.

"Now, one day in 1671, Colonel Blood visited the Tower of London, disguised as a parson."

"A parson?" I said.

"A vicar," said the Queen.

"A vicar?"

"A priest."

"OK," I said.

COL. BLOOD

"Blood brought with him a woman disguised as a parson's wife.

"This woman's name is lost to history, so I will just make one up for her. Wilhelmina."

"Wilhelmina?"

"A good name. Simple."

"Hmmm..." I said. "Can you just make up a name in a true story?" I asked.

"When you're the one telling the story, you can do whatever you want," said the Queen. "Now. Blood put his awful plan into motion. Standing in the Tower of London before those wonderful treasures—crowns and scepters and orbs!—Wilhelmina swooned and fell to the floor!

"'Help!' cried Colonel Blood. 'Someone please help! My wife, Wilhelmina, has fainted dead away!'

"The good Talbot Edwards, Keeper of the Crown Jewels, rushed to her aid. He and Blood carried the woman upstairs, to the Keeper's apartments. Edwards called out to his wife, 'Fetch this poor woman some spirits!'

"On the couch, the patient fluttered her eyes and sat up straight. 'Thank you, good sir! I believe you have saved my life!'

"Colonel Blood clapped Edwards on the back. 'How can we ever repay you?'

"'Oh, parson,' said Edwards. 'There is no need.'

"But the next day Blood returned bearing gifts!"

"What kind of gifts?" I asked.

"Wonderful gifts!" said the Queen. "Gloves!"

"Gloves?" I said.

"Gloves!" said the Queen.

"Hmmm," I said.

"The best gifts are those you can wear," said the Queen.

"No," I said. "The best gifts are those you can read, tied with those you can play—"

"Like a bassoon?" said the Queen.

"Like a Nintendo game," I said. "Followed by those you can play *with*—"

"Like a nanny!"

"Like a Super Soaker. Followed by those you can eat."

"It seems you do a lot of thinking about gifts," said the Queen.

I did. (I still do.) My mom also thought the best gifts were those you could wear, which is why I owned three pairs of overalls and no Super Soakers.

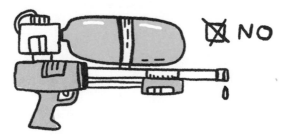

"Anyway," said the Queen, "Colonel Blood, disguised as the parson, gave Edwards the gloves.

'Here, Mr. Edwards, a gift for your wife. Take these four pairs of gloves and—'"

"How many hands does this lady have?" I asked.

"The more gloves, the better the gift," said the Queen. "Everybody knows that.

"The next day Blood came back.

"'My friend, Edwards!' Blood said. 'I'd like to buy your collection of pistols!'

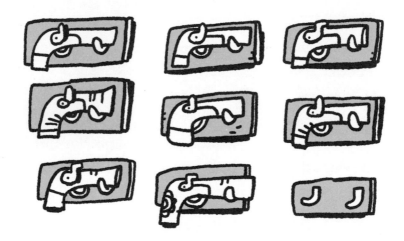

"'My pistols?' Edwards said. 'But they are worthless. I don't think these old guns should fetch very much money.'

"But Blood bought Edwards's pistols and paid a lot of money for them. 'Truly!' said Edwards. 'How my fortunes have changed since I met you, good parson!' Just think! The man had sold his guns for great sums. He was swimming in gloves. 'Now,' Edwards joked, 'if only someone would marry my daughter.'

"Now it was time to spring the trap. Colonel Blood smiled. 'Why sir, I have a rich nephew,' he said, 'who is seeking a wife!'"

"Uh-oh," I said.

"Old Mr. Edwards beamed at the news. 'Well, let us meet this young gentleman! Bring him to dinner!'

"And so one warm spring night, Colonel Blood and two men rode forth to the Tower of London. 'This is my handsome nephew,' said Blood. 'And this other fellow here, with the mallets and sharp knives in his belt, erm, he's my third cousin.' Mrs. Edwards stood in the kitchen, humming a tune and preparing their supper. Young Miss Edwards was upstairs, trying on lovely dresses to look nice for her suitor.

"'Perhaps while we wait,' said Blood, 'you might show my family the Crown Jewels? They would so like to see them.'"

"Oh no," I said.

"Oh yes," said the Queen. "Poor Edwards was only too happy to do it. He fetched his keys and led the men downstairs. And when he unlocked the door to the Jewel Room, Colonel Blood threw his cloak over Edwards's head!

"The men tied up the good Keeper like a sheep in a sack. Then they hit him with mallets."

"This is awful!" I said.

"It is history," said the Queen. "Then they stabbed him."

"Oh, come on!" I exclaimed.

"Colonel Blood hid a crown in the folds of his robe. His nephew stuffed a gold orb down the front of his trousers."

"Ummmmm," I said.

"And the third man set to sawing a scepter in half."

"Why?" I asked.

"Well, so it would fit inside of his trousers," said the Queen.

"But on the floor, under the cloak, battered and stabbed, Edwards cried out: 'Treason! Murder! The Crown Jewels are stolen!' Guards swarmed the tower. The thieves fled for the Thames! 'Fetch my pistols!' cried Edwards. 'They're mounted up on the—oh.'

"Running for the river, Blood fired a pistol (probably one of Edwards's) over his shoulder, but he and his band were tackled before they could get on their horses. And what do you think happened then?"

"They cut off his head?" I asked.

"No, the King forgave Colonel Blood and gave him some nice land in County Meath, Ireland. Nice county."

"But he tried to steal the King's stuff!"

"As I said," said the Queen, "we are all of us a lot of things. Some of them good, some of them bad. Yes, he was a thief, but the man had panache."

"Panache?"

"Style and verve. Colonel Blood possessed swagger, and the King had a soft spot for scoundrels. Besides, the Crown Jewels were fine. A little dinged up, yes, but they were repaired. The story ends happily!"

"What about Edwards?" I asked.

"Oh. Edwards. The King gave him three hundred pounds for his troubles."

"That's *it*?" I asked. "He got stabbed."

"Three hundred pounds was a lot of money back then! Although, now that you mention it, let me have a look at the royal checkbook . . ."

The Queen put on some glasses and dug through her purse. She pulled out a large book.

"Ah. Well. Would you look at that. It appears Edwards was never paid. Oopsie!"

"WHAT!" I said.

"This was before my time!" said the Queen. "Anyway, Edwards got a wonderful story. And isn't a good story the greatest treasure of all?"

"Hmmm," I said.

"I can't believe it," I said.

"Well, it's true," said the Queen. "You can look it up. I spiced up some dialogue, but everything happened, especially the things that are hard to believe."

"The part with the gloves?"

"Yes, the part with the gloves."

"The part where the thieves put the jewels down their pants?"

The Queen grimaced.

"I mean their trousers," I said.

"Indeed," said the Queen.

She looked at me meaningfully.

"Now Mac, the robbery was attempted on May ninth."

"OK," I said.

She continued to look at me meaningfully.

"Why are you looking at me like that?" I asked.
She gestured to the wall, meaningfully.
My eyes went to a calendar.

"Today is May ninth!" I said.

"Indeed," said the Queen.

I looked again at the letter, its threatening red ink.

"It's been three hundred eighteen years exactly," I said.

"And that is why," said the Queen, "tonight Colonel Blood's great-great-great-great-great-great-great-great-great-great grandson will try to steal the Crown Jewels again. Mac, you must stop him!"

If you have read my first book about life as a spy, *Mac Undercover,* you already know what the Tower of London looks like. If you haven't, it looks like this:

And if you read that first book, you already know what beefeaters look like. If you didn't read it, well, maybe you should! Also, beefeaters look like this:

And if you have read the first book (again, it's called *Mac Undercover*), you might remember a beefeater who did not like spies. Here was his face when he met me in the first book:

And here is his face when he saw me again:

"Please stop making that face, Holcroft," said the Queen of England. "It is terribly unattractive." Holcroft made this face instead:

"A little better," said the Queen. "But not much."

We were all three of us—the Queen, Holcroft, and me—standing inside a small white cell. A small table in the center of the room held a crown, a scepter, and an orb.

"Here before you are the items Colonel Blood tried to steal so many centuries ago," said the Queen. "I expect Young Blood will come to steal them tonight."

"What I don't understand," I said, "is why Blood would write you a letter, warning you he was coming for the jewels."

"Well," said the Queen, "when a thief tells someone he's going to steal something and then he steals it, it shows panache. Panache runs in their blood. Oh! Get it? Ha ha! In any case, I took the precaution of order- ing Holcroft to remove these three treasures from the Jewel House and bring them here, to this dungeon. I now entrust them to your care. When I leave this cell, I will lock you both inside. You are to keep watch this night and see to it that Young Blood does not succeed in pilfering my jewels. Tomorrow morning I will come to let you out again. If any attempt is made on my treasures, sound the alarm! Subdue the villain! Stop at nothing to protect the jewels!"

"I like to think I have panache," said Holcroft.

"Holcroft," said the Queen, "you have many fine qualities, but panache is not one of them."

Holcroft gave the Queen a grim nod and gripped his axe.

PUT THAT DOWN.

I nodded too, and wished that I had an axe or something.

Holcroft cleared his throat. "A wonderful plan, ma'am. But with respect, I'd rather not keep watch with him."

The Queen sighed.

"And why not?" she asked.

"Well, ma'am, it's a guardsman's job, watching over the jewels. I don't like spies."

"With respect," I said, "*I'd* rather not keep watch with *him*."

The Queen sighed. "And why not?"

"Because he doesn't like me."

"Listen," said the Queen. "Have you ever tried to stay up all night?"

"Yeah!" I said.

"And what happened?"

"I fell asleep."

"Exactly," said the Queen. "This is a case of two heads being better than one, which is a funny expression to use at this moment, since many people who were locked in this dungeon lost their heads. Ha ha!"

"Hmmm," I said.

"You will sleep in shifts. And you will learn to work together. When two people overcome their differences to succeed at an important task, it provides an important lesson about teamwork, and it is good to always be teaching children important lessons."

"OK," I said.

"But ma'am," said Holcroft.

The Queen frowned and cleared her throat. When she spoke you could tell she was using all capital letters. (My mom had a similar tone of voice.)

"FOLLOW MY COMMAND," said the Queen. "THAT IS AN ORDER!"

Holcroft straightened his back.

"Yes, ma'am," said Holcroft.

He smiled, but you could tell he didn't mean it.

The Queen pulled out a large key ring and stepped outside the cell.

"I am locking you inside now," she said. "Good night, Holcroft! Good night, Mac! Good night, jewels! See you all in the morning!"

The lock clanged, the keys jangled, and the Queen's footsteps grew faint as she disappeared down a winding staircase.

I smiled at Holcroft.

Holcroft glared at me.

I sneezed, and my sneeze echoed against the walls of our cell.

"Well," I said. "This is weird."

Two hours later, the sun had gone down.

Our cell was lit by footlights that cast strange shadows on the wall.

Holcroft was passing time by playing solitaire on the floor.

I wished I had brought a book, or my Game Boy.

"This is kind of like a slumber party!" I said.

"This is nothing like a slumber party," said Holcroft. "Have you ever been to a slumber party?"

"No," I said. "But my friend Derek Lafoy had a few last year and I heard all about them."

Holcroft lost his game and shuffled the cards.

"Hey," I said. "Do you know any two-player games, like old maid?"

"Yes," Holcroft said.

He kept playing solitaire.

I was bored.

My teachers always said I was better at talking to adults than I was to other kids. So I made a try at what grown-ups call "small talk."

"Hey," I said. "Why do they call you guys beef-eaters?"

Holcroft did not look up from his game. "Used to be," he said, "every night, the guards at the Tower ate beef for supper."

"Ah," I said. "Good name."

For the first time Holcroft smiled at me.

"It's a nickname, you know. Our full name is Yeomen Warders of Her Majesty's Royal Palace and Fortress the Tower of London, and Members of the Sovereign's Body Guard of the Yeoman Guard Extraordinary."

YEOMAN WARDER OF HER MAJESTY'S ROYAL PALACE AND FORTRESS THE TOWER OF LONDON, AND MEMBER OF THE SOVEREIGN'S BODY GUARD OF THE YEOMAN GUARD EXTRAORDINARY

YE OLD-TIMEY BUSINESS CARD

"Well, that feels a little long."

Holcroft stopped smiling at me.

"It's an important job, isn't it? Guarding the jewels. Protecting the tower. Seems to me an important job deserves a long name."

"OK," I said.

"*Seems to me*," Holcroft said, "our name could be even longer. Used to be kings and queens slept here, and we protected them too. Used to be, notorious prisoners were locked up in these very towers, and we made sure they didn't escape. That's honorable work!"

"OK," I said.

"I take this seriously," Holcroft said. "Members of my family've been Yeomen Warders of Her Majesty's Royal Palace and Fortress the Tower of London, and Members of the Sovereign's Body Guard of the Yeoman Guard Extraordinary going back twelve generations! And I don't need some American kid spy telling me whether the name's any good!"

"OK," I said.

The cell was silent.

"Well," I said, "who wants to sleep first?"

Holcroft held out a gold coin.

"Heads or tails," he said. "Loser takes the first watch."

He flipped the coin in the air.

"Tails!" I said.

I had a rule: Always call tails.

The coin clanged on the floor, danced on its edge, and fell.

It was heads.

Staring up from the coin, the Queen looked disappointed in me.

"You lose," Holcroft said. "Wake me up in four hours."

He lay down on the floor and pulled his cloak over his head.

"You're just sleeping right there?"

"A soldier can sleep anywhere," he said from under the cloak.

"Neat," I said. "Well, good night."

He peeled back the cloak. "Don't fall asleep."

"I know," I said.

"You have to stay focused. Don't let your mind get away from you."

"I *know*," I said.

"If your mind starts to wander, make a list of everything that's in the room. It's an old soldier's trick."

"Good night!" I said.

Holcroft started snoring.

My mind started wandering.

My eyes started closing.

No!

I forced them back open.

I had to prove to Holcroft I could stay awake for my shift.

I yawned.

It was me versus my mind.

I did like Holcroft said and looked around the room.

That's it.

This was a small room.
I did it again.
A table.
A crown.
A scepter.
An orb.
A man.
An axe.
Me.
I checked my watch. Only a minute had passed.
I had to look closer.
(A good spy notices everything.)
A spider.

A web.

Four walls made of stone. No! Made of stones!
I'd count every stone! That would take me hours!
I would start from the top. One, two, three, four,
five, six, seven, eight, nine, ten, eleven, twelve,
thirteen, fourteen, fifteen, sixteen, seventeen,
eighteen, nineteen, twenty, twenty-one, twenty-two,
twenty-three, twenty-four, twenty-five, twenty-six,
twenty-seven, twenty-eight, twenty-nine, thirty,
thirty-one, thirty-two, thirty-three, thirty-four, thirty-
five, thirty-six, thirty-seven, thirty-eight, thirty-nine,
forty, forty-one, forty-two, forty-three, forty-four,
forty-five, forty-six, forty-seven, forty-eight, forty-
nine, fifty, fifty-one, fifty-two, fifty-three, fifty-four,

fifty-five, fifty-six, fifty-seven, fifty-eight, fifty-nine, sixty, sixty-one, sixty-two, sixty-three, sixty-four, sixty-five, sixty-six, sixty-seven, sixty-eight, sixty-nine, seventy, seventy-one, seventy-two, seventy-three, seventy-four, seventy-five, seventy-six, seventy-seven, seventy-eight, seventy-nine, eighty, eighty-one, eighty-two, eighty-three, eighty-four, eighty-five, eighty-six, eighty-seven, eighty-eight, eighty-nine, ninety, ninety-one, ninety-two, ninety-three, ninety-four, ninety-five, ninety-six, ninety-seven, ninety-eight, ninety-nine, one hundred, one hundred one, one hundred two, one hundred three, one hundred four, one hundred five, one hundred six, one hundred seven, one hundred eight, one hundred nine, one hundred ten, one hundred

eleven, one hundred twelve, one hundred thirteen, one hundred fourteen, one hundred fifteen, one hundred sixteen, one hundred seventeen, one hundred eighteen, one hundred nineteen, one hundred twenty, one hundred twenty-one, one hundred twenty-two, one hundred twenty-three, one hundred twenty-four, one hundred twenty-five, one hundred twenty-six, one hundred twenty-seven, one hundred twenty-eight, one hundred twenty-nine, one hundred thirty, one hundred thirty-one, one hundred thirty-two, one hundred thirty-three, one hundred thirty-four, one hundred thirty-five, one hundred thirty-six, one hundred thirty-seven, one hundred thirty-eight, one hundred thirty-nine, one hundred forty, one hundred forty-one, one

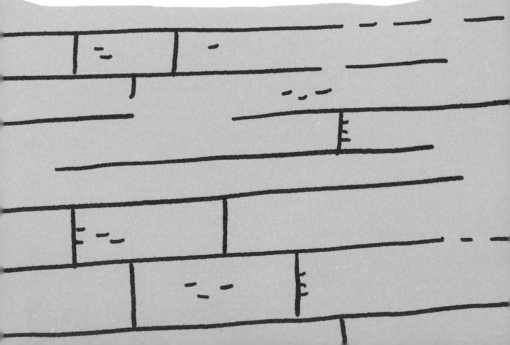

hundred forty-two, one hundred forty-three, one hundred forty-four, one hundred forty-five, one hundred forty-six, one hundred forty-seven, one hundred forty-eight, one hundred forty-nine, one hundred fifty, one hundred fifty-one, one hundred fifty-two, one hundred fifty-three, one hundred fifty-four, one hundred fifty-five, one hundred fifty-six, one hundred fifty-seven, one hundred fifty-eight, one hundred fifty-nine, one hundred sixty, one hundred fifty-sixty-one, one hundred sixty-two, one hundred sixty-three, one hundred sixty-four, one hundred sixty-five, one hundred sixty-six, one hundred sixty-seven, one hundred sixty-eight, one hundred sixty-nine, one hundred seventy, one hundred seventy-one, one hundred seventy-two, one hundred seventy-three, one hundred seventy-four, one hundred seventy-five, one hundred seventy-six, one hundred seventy-seven, one hundred seventy-eight, one hundred seventy-nine, one hundred eighty, one hundred eighty-one, one hundred eighty-two, one hundred eighty-three, one hundred eighty-four, one hundred eighty-five, one hundred eighty-six, one hundred eighty-seven, one hundred eighty-eight, one hundred eighty-nine, one hundred ninety, one hundred ninety-one, one hundred ninety-two, one hundred ninety-three, one hundred ninety-four, one hundred ninety-five, one hundred ninety-six, one hundred ninety-seven, one hundred ninety-eight, one hundred ninety-nine, two hundred, two hundred one, two hundred two, two hundred three, two hundred four, two hundred five, two hundred six, two hundred seven, two hundred eight, two hundred nine, two hundred ten, two hundred eleven, two hundred twelve, two hundred thirteen, two hundred fourteen, two hundred fifteen, two hundred sixteen, two hundred seventeen, two hundred eighteen, two hundred nineteen, two hundred twenty, two hundred twenty-one, two hundred twenty-two, two hundred twenty-three—

As you now know, counting stones is boring. On stone 223 I fell fast asleep.

Holcroft was shaking me hard.

I opened my eyes.

"You fool!" Holcroft shouted. "You ninny! You cloaf!"

"What?" I said. "Holcroft, what's wrong?"

"You fell asleep."

I checked my watch.

"Just for a few minutes."

"That was enough."

I took a look at the table.

The Crown Jewels were gone.

I scrambled to my feet. "We must look for clues."

"There's no time!" Holcroft said. "We have to give chase!"

He ran to the cell door.

It was still locked.

"Cripes!" he shouted. "We're trapped in this cell!"

Holcroft rattled the bars and shouted into the dark.

"The Crown Jewels are stolen!"

The Queen of England was unhappy.

"Mac fell asleep," said Holcroft.

"Yes," said the Queen. "This is very disappointing."

She thought for a second.

"However, this is also very exciting!"

"Ma'am?" Holcroft said.

"We are in the middle of a mystery. And not just a *normal* mystery! It's a howdunit!" said the Queen.

"Don't you mean a whodunit?" I said.

"Of course not," said the Queen. "We already know who done it. Young Blood done it."

"Don't you mean *did* it?" I said.

"Please do not correct me," said the Queen. "It's called the Queen's English for a reason."

"OK."

"We also know Young Blood's motive." The Queen waved the red letter around in the air. "He wanted to get what his great-great-great-great-great-great-great-great-great grandfather did not. And so: It is not a whydunit."

"Ah," said Holcroft. "Quite so."

"It is not a whendunit. It was done just now, while Mac was sleeping on the job. That was the criminal's opportunity."

"Sorry," I said.

"Thus," said the Queen, "it is a howdunit! We must figure out how Young Blood done what he done! How could he steal jewels from a cell without breaking the bars? It's an impossible crime!"

"Not impossible," I said. "Just really, really hard."

The Queen clapped her hands together.

"I simply love a locked-room mystery!"

"Me too!" I said.

(I did. I still do.)

"Oh!" said the Queen. "Do you know any good ones?"

"Yeah," I said. "There's one in Paris where—"

"I know it already," said the Queen. "The ape went up the chimney."

"Oh," I said. "Well there's one where this guy who builds all these robots—"

"He dressed up as a postman," said the Queen.

"All right," I said. "Do you know the one where the guy goes to the supermarket for two bottles of relish?"

"That one is absolutely revolting," said the Queen. "It is my favorite."

"OK," I said. "Well here's one I heard the other day. Police find a dead man in a locked room, hanged from the ceiling with a rope around his neck—"

"Cripes!" said Holcroft. "Seems a bit grim for a little boy, doesn't it? All this hanging?"

"I don't know," I said. "It's just a story. Everyone at school does these riddles at recess all the time."

Holcroft was aghast.

(Most adults don't have any idea of what happens on playgrounds. You probably already know that's true without looking it up.)

"Oh, let him get on with it," said the Queen of England.

"Police find a dead man in a locked room, hanged from the ceiling with a rope around his neck. The ceiling in this room is twenty feet high, which, you know, is very high."

"Sounds like normal ceiling height to me," said the Queen of England. "Many of the rooms in my house are at least twenty feet tall."

"Well, anyway, the police can't figure out how this guy got up there. Then the detective notices a puddle of water on the floor. 'I know what happened!' the detective says."

"What happened?" shouted the Queen. "What happened?"

"Don't you want to figure it out yourself?" I said.

"No!" said the Queen.

"It's more fun if you try to figure it out."

"Just tell me the answer!"

"OK," I said. "The man stood on a giant block of ice to hang himself, and then it melted."

"Ah!" said the Queen. "Excellent!"

"Wait. How'd he do that?" said Holcroft.

"What?"

"How'd he get on top of the block?" said Holcroft. "Pretty tough to scramble up a fifteen-foot ice cube."

I'd heard this riddle a hundred times and never thought of that.

"Well," I said, "maybe there were steps carved into the ice block."

"Steps!" said Holcroft.

"Yeah, maybe it was an ice staircase."

Holcroft rolled his eyes. "Oh, yes, of course. An ice staircase."

"Yeah," I said. "Maybe the guy was an ice sculptor."

Holcroft blew a raspberry.

I shook my head. "You don't get it."

"You're right. I *don't* get it."

"It's just a riddle," I said. "Right, Your Majesty?"

"Indeed," said the Queen. "But what occurred last night is a *real life* locked-room mystery. It actually happened. I must know the solution!"

"OK," I said. I looked back around the cell. "Let me think."

"I cannot wait around while you think," said the Queen. "I have to know now! Just go get the answer!"

"From who?" I said.

"I think you mean from *whom*," said the Queen. "From Young Blood, of course! Go get him, arrest him, and make him tell how he did it! And fetch back my jewels while you're at it."

"Go get him where?" I said.

"I told you yesterday," the Queen said. "The King of England gave the Bloods land in Ireland. Go! Holcroft, ready the helicopter."

"But ma'am," Holcroft said, "I can do this myself."

"You are working together! Remember: team-work and cooperation!"

"But," I said, "if I could just search this cell for some clues!"

"Mac," said the Queen, "you are not a detective. You are a secret agent. So stop looking for clues and go sneak into another country to nab a bad guy."

"But—" said Holcroft.

The Queen frowned and cleared her throat.

"GO!" said the Queen. "THAT IS AN ORDER!"

"Yes, ma'am," said Holcroft.

And we went.

Ireland is a country with no snakes and lots of castles.

The big reason Ireland has so many castles is that it is an island, and islands tend to attract invaders. Castles are a good way to repel invaders. Over the centuries, Ireland has been invaded by

And lots of Americans who are part Irish and want to visit, like me!

There is a story about why Ireland does not have any snakes. The story is that a bunch of snakes swarmed a man name Saint Patrick while he was thinking under a tree, and he got so mad that he drove all the snakes in Ireland into the ocean. This story is not true, but Saint Patrick got his own holiday anyway. (You can look that up.)

The big reason Ireland doesn't have any snakes is that it is an island, and although snakes are excellent invaders, they cannot sail boats or fly helicopters.

Our helicopter flew in the darkness, over the sea.

I looked down and saw dark green pastures dotted with horses, dark green fields dotted with barley, and dark green lawns dotted with castles.

Holcroft landed the helicopter on a castle's front lawn.

"Here we are," Holcroft said.

We walked up some steps to the castle's huge entrance.

I wiped my feet on a gigantic doormat.

"Pardon," Holcroft said, and nudged me aside. He lifted a corner of the doormat and pulled out a gigantic key ring.

"The Plunketts are out of town," he said. "They told Her Majesty the Queen we could stay at their castle."

He unlocked the front door. It creaked on its hinges.

"The Plunketts?" I said.

"Baron and Baroness Plunkett own Dunsany Castle."

(I know those sound like fake names. But they're not. You can look them up.)

The castle was empty and damp and too big. Moonlight shone weakly through tall peaked windows.

"This place is creepy," I said.

"It's convenient," Holcroft said. "The Bloods' land is nearby. Get some rest. We'll go get Young Blood in the morning."

The wind moaned as it passed through a high tower.

"We're sleeping here?" I said. "It feels like it's haunted."

"A soldier can sleep anywhere," Holcroft said. "Good night."

He climbed up a staircase and disappeared into a room.

I searched the castle for a good place to sleep.

I didn't like the look of the bed in one room.
And the grandfather clock in another looked a
bit suspicious.

I settled on sleeping in the library.

I always felt safer surrounded by books.

(I still do.)

It was a great red room, with thick velvet drapes and an oversized fireplace.

I looked out the windows and thought I saw shadows move in the fog.

Did Young Blood know we were here?

Was he coming to stop us?

I pulled the drapes closed and locked the door to the room.

I turned on a lamp.

What I saw made me scream!

It was a tiger!

Well, it was a tiger-skin rug, laid out by the hearth. Its fur was white with black stripes. Its eyes shone in the lamplight. It had lots of teeth.

"Yikes," I said.

It was pretty awful.

I decided not to look at that part of the room.

I turned to my right.

What I saw made me scream!

It was another tiger-skin rug.

This one had a chessboard placed right on its back.

"Double yikes," I said.

I started to think I'd chosen a bad room to sleep in.

Still, I made a nice fire.

I took down a book from the shelf and lay down on a rug.

(A regular rug. Not one made from a tiger.)

I read till I got drowsy.

Then I fell asleep, sprawled out on the floor like a tiger-skin rug.

I dreamed something soft was tickling my belly.

I awoke with a start.

What I saw made me scream!

It was a cobra!

Not a cobra-skin rug.

There is no such thing.

A real live king cobra was coiled on my chest.

Its scales were white with black flecks.

When I screamed, it reared up.

The cobra hissed.

I tried to think of everything I knew about snakes.

I knew that I was afraid of snakes.

I knew that if this cobra bit me I would probably die.

I knew that Derek Lafoy said he hypnotized his pet snake every night by crossing his eyes at it.

So I tried that.

The cobra's hood flew open, which seemed like a bad thing.

It hissed again.

As the cobra started to strike, the phone rang.

The cobra swung its head toward the table and bit its leg. The table's leg. Not the cobra's leg. Cobras don't have legs, but tables do. (That's true. You can look it up.)

I rolled toward the fireplace and picked up a poker, then rushed to the table and pinned the snake to the ground.

"Got you!" I said.

The snake hissed again.

The door to the library flew open.

Holcroft, in pajamas, rushed in with his axe.

Our eyes met.

"Did it bite you?" he asked.

I shook my head no.

"Ah," said Holcroft. "Good."

Holcroft set a priceless urn upside down over the snake. "Got him."

"What're you going to do with it?" I asked.

Now, if you were hoping this deadly snake was going to be released into the wild and start a snake family, you might want to read a different kind of story, where only nice things happen, like *The Day Our Substitute Teacher Changed Our Lives*, or *Grandma, Tell Me about Your Locket*.

But this is a Secret Agent story. (Besides, there are very strict laws about releasing snakes into Ireland. That's true. You can look it up.)

"Tomorrow I shall drop him in the ocean, like Saint Patrick."

"Oh man," I said.

"By the way," said Holcroft, "are you going to answer that?"

The phone was still ringing.

My hand was shaking when I answered the call.

"Hello," I said.

"Hullo," said the Queen of England. "May I speak to Mac?"

"Speaking," I said.

"Mac!" said the Queen. "How are things going?"

"Not great," I said. "A snake just tried to kill me."

"A snake?" said the Queen. "I think you're mistaken. There are no snakes in Ireland."

"Well, it was definitely a snake. Somebody must have brought it here."

Holcroft said, "Tell her Young Blood must be trying to kill us!"

"You mean he's trying to kill me," I said.

"Well I'm sure I was next," Holcroft said. "Young Blood just started with the easy one first."

"No," I said. "You start with the important one first. Everybody knows that."

"Please!" said the Queen. "It's rude to talk to someone else while you're on the phone."

My mom always hated when I did that too.

"Sorry," I said.

"You are forgiven," said the Queen. "Now. Did the snake bite you?"

"No," I said. "Holcroft put it under a priceless urn."

"Aha!" said the Queen. "Holcroft saved your life!"

"Not really," I said. "I already had the snake trapped."

"Ingrate," Holcroft said.

"I can sense the two of you growing closer and closer. By the end of this mission, you'll be best chums. I know it."

"Hmmm," I said.

"Anyway, I'm sorry to ring up so late. I'm having some trouble getting to sleep. My mind won't quiet down. I wonder, do you know any more of those riddles?"

"Sure," I said. "You're trapped in a locked room."

"Oh dear," said the Queen.

"The only thing in the room is a table and an axe. How do you get out?"

"Chop through the walls!" said the Queen. "Easy!"

"The walls are made of stone."

"Why, Mac! If you can explain how to escape from a stone room with only a table and an axe, you can solve the mystery of my Crown Jewels! There was a table and an axe in the cell with you that evening! You've cracked the case! The answer was inside you all along! Tell me, what is the solution?"

"Ummm," I said. "Well. You use the axe to chop the table in half. Two halves make a whole, so you climb through the hole and escape."

The line was silent for a while.

"What?" said the Queen.

"It's a play on words. Whole and hole."

"But you cannot climb through a whole," said the Queen.

"Right, I mean, I don't know. It's wordplay."

"That's a terrible riddle," said the Queen.

"Yeah," I said. "It's not the best one. If anything, it's more of a joke."

"Yes," said the Queen. "And it's a terrible joke."

"OK," I said.

"I cannot believe I wasted the time and money placing this phone call. Night night. Don't let the cobras bite."

She hung up.

The phone rang again.

I answered.

"Now *that* was a good joke," said the Queen.

She chuckled, then hung up again.

Holcroft stood in the doorway, cleaning his axe.

"Two halves make a hole?" He shook his head.

I closed the door on his face and locked it.

It was hard getting back to sleep, with a deadly snake rattling around in a priceless urn in the corner. So in the early hours of the morning, I left the castle and walked down a country road.

I don't know how long I walked, past paddocks and barns and crumbling stone walls.

The sky grew lighter.

My mind kept returning to the mystery of the tower cell.

How had Young Blood done it?

Broken into the room and escaped with the jewels.
The cell contained only
a table,
a crown,
a scepter,
an orb,
a man,
an axe,
and me.
I stuffed my hands in my pockets and kicked gravel while I walked.
A table,
a crown,
a scepter,
an orb,
a man,
an axe,
me.
I became lost in the problem. When I looked up again, I was in a small village.
I paused by a graveyard and sat down on a bench.
I had a pen and a notebook in my jeans' front pocket.
I always carried paper and pen.
(I still do.)

I wrote down my list, the one stuck in my head.

I looked at my list and thought hard.

The sun rose in the east.

Birds started to chirp.

A faint plinking came from somewhere nearby.

The walls were too thick to cut through.

The windows were high off the ground and too narrow to pass through.

Unless the thief were a monkey!

But that didn't feel right.

I thought and I thought.

Nearby, someone or something plinked and plinked.

I stared at the paper.

I looked up at the sky.

The answer danced somewhere at the edge of my mind.

Plink, plink, plink.

"What is that noise?" I shouted.

I stood up abruptly and startled a sparrow.

Plink, plink, plink.

It came from a little white house on the edge of the graveyard.

I could not think with this plinking.

It had to be stopped.

The plinking got louder as I approached.

I ducked around the back of the house, toward the source of the plinks.

I turned the corner.

I came face-to-face with an old man raising an ice pick over his head! There was a mad gleam in his eye as he brought the ice pick down hard!

I should probably say that between me and the man there was a large block of ice.

Plink!

"Excuse me, sir," I said. "But what in the heck are you doing?"

The old man lowered his pick and smiled at me. "Making ice sculptures, lad."

I saw then that his backyard was full of things carved from ice.

Several ice swans.
An ice castle.
An ice windmill.
An ice Lamborghini.

The one he was working on now curved round and round and rose high in the air, like a cobra about to strike.

"Well," I said, "do you think you could please keep it down? I'm a secret agent, and I'm trying to solve a tough case."

The man did not stop smiling.

"I'm sorry, son. But I have an important job too. I've got to finish these sculptures by noon today. I've been working all night. The Plunketts come back today. They're having a party up at their castle."

"Oh!" I said. "That's where I'm staying."

The old man looked surprised. "Creepy place," he said.

"Very creepy!" I said.

"The kind of place where you'd better sleep with your doors locked, as the old expression goes!"

"I did lock my door!" I said. "And I have never heard that expression!"

The old man resumed carving.

Plink, plink, plink.

"Well," he said, "why don't you tell me all about your case."

"Well, it's top secret so I probably shouldn't," I said. "But maybe you can help! Someone stole the

Queen of England's Crown Jewels from a locked cell in the Tower of London!"

The old man shook his head and spat on the ground.

"Well then, I'm afraid I can't be much help. For one thing, I'm not fond of English queens. For another, I don't much like locked-room mysteries."

"You don't?"

"No," said the man. "A question's always more exciting than an answer. Who sees a magician make an elephant vanish, then wants to know how it's done?"

"Me!" I said.

The old man frowned. "Mirrors, mostly. And misdirection. The magician tells you to look over there, so you don't pay attention to what's important."

"Oh," I said. "Well that's kind of a letdown."

"When a mystery's unsolved, the impossible is possible. Take your case. The missing jewels. Maybe your thief had a shrink ray and climbed through the keyhole. Or maybe the jewels are still in the cell, but they're invisible."

"A shrink ray!" I said.

"Yes! But it won't be a shrink ray," said the old man. "When you solve the mystery, it'll be some simple explanation, one that's been in front of your face the whole time. It'll be just mirrors and misdirection."

"Oh."

"I say it's better to live with the impossible than demand answers for everything."

"Yeah," I said. "But a secret agent's job is to answer questions."

"Then maybe you ought to look for a new job," said the man. "One where you get to ask them."

He smiled at me cryptically.

"Well," he said, "I've got to get back to work. If you're looking for quiet, you may want to find a new graveyard. I'll be at it all morning."

"What are you carving?"

"An ice staircase," he said.

"Oh," I said. "I thought it might be a giant snake."

He spat again.

"I dislike snakes even more than I dislike English queens."

"I don't like snakes either," I said. "Someone tried to kill me last night by putting a cobra in my room."

"Ah," said the old man, "the life of a spy."

126

"I guess," I said.

"Another good reason to change jobs," said the old man. "Well, you best get to thinking, while I get to plinking. It sounds like you've got *two* locked-room mysteries to solve."

"What?"

"You said you locked the door to your room. How'd the snake get in?"

I stared at the old man.

Then I looked down at my notebook.

"I know how he done it," I said.

"How who done it?" said the old man.

"Thank you, sir," I said.

My heart was beating fast.

"Please," said the old man, "don't call me sir. It makes me feel old."

He held out his hand.

"The name's Blood. Jerry Blood."

COL. BLOOD!   JERRY BLOOD!

I ran to the village and dropped some Irish coins in a phone.

It rang three times before someone picked up.

"Hullo?" someone said.

"Hello," I said. "May I speak to the Queen?"

"Speaking," she said.

"You need to come to Ireland, quick."

22

WHODUNIT

    In the library of Dunsany Castle, fourteen of us gathered: me, Holcroft, the Queen, and eleven corgis.

    "They love to travel!" the Queen said.

    Freddie was licking the head of a tiger-skin rug.

    I cleared my throat.

    "You're probably wondering why I've gathered you here together," I said.

    "So you can reveal the solution to the mystery," said the Queen. "Obviously."

"Oh," I said. "Well, yes."

"What a silly thing to say," said the Queen.

"I thought it showed panache," I said.

"No, that's not panache."

"OK," I said. "Well, anyway, I give you . . . Young Blood!"

I gestured to the velvet drapes by the window.

Jerry Blood threw the curtains aside and stepped forward.

"Hello," he said.

"What an entrance!" said the Queen. "Now *that's* panache."

Jerry Blood smiled.

I rolled my eyes.

"I must say," said the Queen, "I thought he'd be younger."

"Well, I'm the youngest one living," he said. "I'm the last of the line."

"I see," said the Queen. "Holcroft, put this villain in chains and haul him away."

"Wait!" I cried.

"Oh, yes!" The Queen clapped her hands. "I almost forgot. How did you do it?"

"Do what?" Young Blood asked.

"Steal my jewels," the Queen said.

Blood shrugged. "I didn't."

"You are a thief," the Queen said.

"I'm not," answered Blood.

"You attempted to murder my secret agent, Mac, which is just as bad."

"Worse," I said.

"I didn't do that either."

"But worst of all," said the Queen, "you are a liar. Lock him up!"

"Your Majesty," I said, "Blood's telling the truth. He didn't steal the jewels. This case was a whodunit after all!"

"Then who done it?" said the Queen. "And also, how?"

I nodded.

"The *how* was in front of my face all along, while I was looking in all the wrong places. Here is a list of all the things in that cell."

I held up my notebook.

"A table, a crown, a scepter, an orb, a man, an axe, and me. That's all that was there before I fell asleep. The cell's walls were thick. The windows were small. The lock was strong. But what if the thief didn't need to break in?"

"I don't get it," the Queen said.

"Neither do I," Holcroft added.

"I don't get it either," said Blood, "if anyone cares."

"What if the thief was already inside? A table, a crown, a scepter, an orb, a man, an axe, and me."

"It was you!" the Queen said. "Holcroft, arrest this child!"

"Gladly," Holcroft said.

"Wait!" I said. "It wasn't me either!"

"Oh dear," said the Queen. "Just tell us who done it."

"Holcroft done it!" I said.

I pointed at the beefeater.

"Outrageous!" Holcroft said.

The Queen frowned. "I must say, I agree. Why would Holcroft do such a thing? Holcroft *guards* the jewels. His family's been beefeaters going back twelve generations."

"Precisely," I said. "Your Majesty, would you please read the threatening letter you got one more time?"

"Gladly."

The Queen put on her glasses.

TOMORROW NIGHT I WILL GET WHAT MY GREAT-GREAT-GREAT-GREAT-GREAT-GREAT-GREAT-GREAT-GREAT GRANDFATHER DID NOT. I WILL NOT BE STOPPED. WE HAVE BEEN WAITING 318 YEARS!

"Holcroft," I said, "what is your last name?"

"I just presumed his last name was Holcroft," said the Queen.

"It's Edwards," Holcroft said. "Holcroft Edwards."

"Aha!" I shouted.

The Queen shrugged. "So what?"

"Holcroft's great-great-great-great-great-great-great-great-great grandfather was Talbot Edwards," I said. "The man who was stabbed stopping Blood and never paid by the King!"

The Queen broke into applause.

Then she stopped clapping suddenly.

"That's the whodunit," she said. "And the whydunit too. But how about the how? How did Holcroft get the jewels out of the cell while you slept? When you woke up, the Crown Jewels were gone."

"No," I said. "They were still in the room."

"They were not!" said the Queen. "The table was bare!"

"That's because Holcroft had stuffed them down the front of his pants!"

The Queen looked horrified.

"Sorry," I said. "Down the front of his trousers."

"Of course!" said the Queen.

"Wow," said Blood, in the corner.

"Ma'am," Holcroft said, "this is outrageous! How can you believe a thing this little brat says? This is a bundle of lies! I'm sorry, ma'am, for what I do next."

Holcroft undid his belt.

His pants fell to the floor.

I mean his trousers.

"There are no jewels hidden here!"

The Queen looked back at me.

"He's right," she said. "Mac, what say you to this?"

"I mean, he didn't keep them in his trousers. He probably hid them in his room here or something."

"Ah," said the Queen. "Yes, that makes more sense. Freddie!"

Freddie ran to the Queen.
She pulled a large diamond out of her purse.
Freddie sniffed it.

He licked it.
He wagged his tail.
"Go find more of these, Freddie!"
He gave a sharp bark and ran out of the room.
"Outrageous!" Holcroft said.
He ran for the door!
But his way out was blocked by ten growling corgis.

The Queen raised her head high.

"Be careful. They bite. We shall wait in this room until Freddie returns."

We stood there a long time.

"Can I go?" asked Blood.

"In a minute," said the Queen.

Five minutes passed.

"By the way," said the Queen, "what is that knocking noise coming from the corner of the room?"

"That's the cobra," I said.

"I see," said the Queen.

Ten minutes passed.

"You know, Holcroft," I said, "you can pull up your pants."

The Queen sighed.

"I mean trousers," I said.

"Oh, quite right," Holcroft said.

Fifty-five minutes later, Freddie came back with the crown!

"Freddie is easily distracted," the Queen explained. Freddie wagged with the crown in his mouth.

The orb and the scepter were found in Holcroft's room.

Freddie couldn't carry all three.

Corgis have very small mouths.

That's true. You can look it up.

"He done it!" cried the Queen.

Holcroft's face flushed bright red, so it looked like his scarlet coat continued right up his neck.

He turned to me and brandished his axe.

"You!" said Holcroft. "You ruined everything!"

I backed into a corner of the library as Holcroft slowly came toward me.

His expression was twisted, mad with rage.

I tried to stop Holcroft by pulling books off the shelf and throwing them at his head, but unfortunately the section I was in contained only paperback mysteries.

Holcroft licked the blade of his axe.

"Mmmmm, *ice cold*!" he said.

The Queen laughed.

"I don't get it," I said.

"That's panache," she said. "I didn't know you had it in you, Holcroft!"

I held a flimsy orange book before me like a tiny shield.

The Queen frowned and cleared her throat.

"HOLCROFT, PLACE YOURSELF UNDER ARREST," said the Queen. "THAT IS AN ORDER."

Holcroft straightened his back. "Yes, ma'am," he said.

He dropped his axe and handcuffed himself to the radiator.

The Queen straightened her crown, turned to me, and smiled. "Well, that's sorted."

"Well, that was certainly interesting," she said.

There was no doubt about it. She had panache.

"I should never have presumed the thief was Blood," said the Queen. "It is just like my father, the King of England, used to say: When you presume, you make a 'pres' out of 'u' and 'me.'"

"A pres?" I asked.

"A president," said the Queen. "And I am no president. I am a *queen*."

The Queen looked at a fancy watch on her wrist.

"Well, it's getting late! I suppose there is no point in returning home before the Plunketts' party, is there? They always serve such wonderful food, and this time they have commissioned a, what did you call it, *mini-golf course*—out of ice! I don't have an invitation, but I am sure they would be delighted if I attended. We'll crash their party!"

"Another English invasion," said Blood.

"What did he just say?" said the Queen.

"Hey, do you think I could come too?" I asked.

"Why not?" said the Queen. "The more, the merrier!"

"Typical," said Blood.

And so:

We all played a game of mini-golf in Ireland

while Holcroft played a game of solitaire in jail.

And then I played my Game Boy on a long flight home.

When I got back, my mom was happy to see me.

"You're missing a lot of school," she said, "doing all these missions for the Queen."

"It's OK," I said. "I have straight As in every-thing."

"Except handwriting," she said.

"I'm working on that."

There was a package for me on the kitchen counter.

It was from the Queen of England.

Dear Agent Mac,

Enclosed you will find a note for your teacher, explaining your absence, as well as a reward to thank you for your service to me, the Queen of England. Hullo from all of us in Britain, except Holcroft, who swears he will be revenged. Ah well!

My Majesty,
The Queen of England

There was an envelope addressed to my teacher and a box wrapped in red paper and tied with a gold bow.

I opened the box.

Inside there were five pairs of gloves.

Plus a note from the Queen.

FIVE
PAIRS'
WORTH
OF
THANKS!

I tried on a pair.

They didn't look great.

Just then the phone rang.

I ran to the living room and picked it up.

"Hello?" I said.

"Hullo," said the Queen. "May I speak to Mac?"

"Speaking," I said.

"Mac, I meant to ask. How did you do it? How did you crack the case?"

"The snake," I said. "When I went to sleep that night, I locked the library door. So how did the snake get into my room? Not through the chimney— the fireplace was lit. And not through the windows— they were sealed shut. Then I realized—someone must have brought the snake in through the library door."

"But you locked it," the Queen said.

"Yes. That's how I knew it was Holcroft. He had the keys to the house. And he came in to trap the snake without breaking the door down."

"Yes, but why trap it? Why save your life?"

"He didn't," I said. "I told you, he only came in once I had the snake caught. He was trying to look innocent, because he was guilty. I'm just lucky I solved the case before he was able to stop me."

"Indeed," said the Queen. "So he just unlocked the door. Well, that's a very disappointing solution to a locked-room mystery."

"That happens sometimes," I said.

"Nevertheless," said the Queen. "I feel terrible for putting you in such great danger."

"Thanks," I said.

"However," she continued, "I'm about to do so again. Mac, I need a favor."

I smiled.

"OK."

THE

END

Mac Barnett is a *New York Times* bestselling author of children's books and a former ████████████. His books have received awards such as the Caldecott Honor, the E. B. White Read Aloud Award, and the Boston Globe-Horn Book Award. His secret agent work has received awards such as the Medal of ████████████, the Cross of ████████████, and the Royal Order of ████████████ ████████████ the Third. His favorite color is ████████. His favorite food is ████████. He lives in Oakland, California. (That's true. You can look it up.)

Mike Lowery used to get in trouble for doodling in his books, and now he's doing it for a living. His drawings have been seen in dozens of books for kids and adults, and on everything from greeting cards to food trucks. He also likes to collect weird little bits of knowledge and recently collected them in his book, *Random Illustrated Facts*. Mike lives in Atlanta, Georgia, with a little German lady and two genius kids.

LOOK OUT FOR THE NEXT

MAC B. KID SPY

ADVENTURE:

TOP-SECRET
SMACKDOWN

Out in
September
2019!

Praise For
MAC UNDERCOVER

A riotous series debut . . . should snare even the most hesitant readers.
—PUBLISHERS WEEKLY

*Barnett takes his readers on a fun-filled ride . . . An enjoyable
romp that will leave readers salivating for the sequel.*
—KIRKUS REVIEWS